The Break-In

Written by Heather Carroll
Illustrated by Sari Richter

Library and Archives Canada Cataloguing in Publication

Carroll, Heather, 1964-
    The break-in / author, Heather Carroll ; illustrator, Sari
Richter.

Short stories.
ISBN 978-0-9881435-1-7

    I. Richter, Sari II. Title.

PS8605.A77725B73 2013   jC813'.6   C2013-901041-6

For information: heathercarrollbooks.ca

First edition
Published and printed in Canada

This is a work of fiction. Names, characters, places, and incidents are either the product of the author's imagination or are used fictitiously, and any resemblance to business establishments, events, locales, or actual persons, living or dead, is entirely coincidental.

This book was written, edited and published by the author. TRIMATRIX assumes no responsibility for damages, direct or indirect, from publication of the included works. Work is included as provided by the author, views expressed are those of the author and any errors, omissions or otherwise are the author's responsibility.

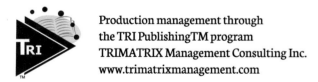
Production management through
the TRI PublishingTM program
TRIMATRIX Management Consulting Inc.
www.trimatrixmanagement.com

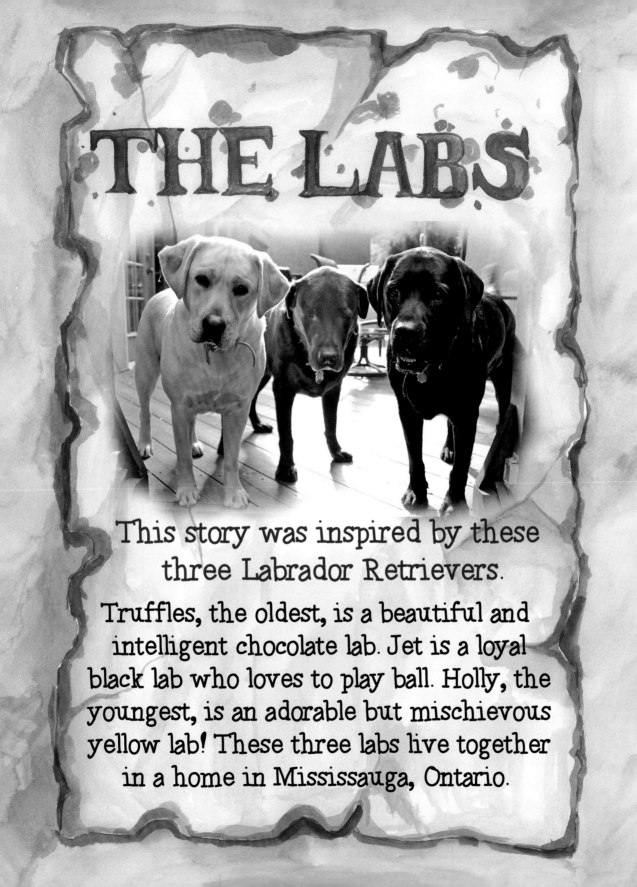

THE LABS

This story was inspired by these three Labrador Retrievers.

Truffles, the oldest, is a beautiful and intelligent chocolate lab. Jet is a loyal black lab who loves to play ball. Holly, the youngest, is an adorable but mischievous yellow lab! These three labs live together in a home in Mississauga, Ontario.

Truffles, Jet and Holly waited eagerly by the front door for Linda to arrive. They were excited because they knew Linda was coming to take them to the dog park.

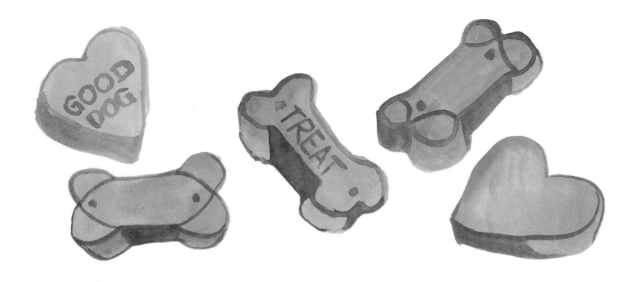

When Linda's van pulled up in front of the house, Truffles, Jet and Holly jumped inside with all their dog friends. Tails were wagging and dogs were barking as the van drove down the street.

When they arrived at the dog park, the day seemed as normal as any other day. The three labs began happily racing around chasing balls, greeting other dogs and rolling in the sand pit.

Then Holly caught a glimpse of an old soccer ball hidden in the bushes. Holly loved soccer balls! She was so excited that she raced toward the ball and sunk her teeth into it.

When she looked up, Holly could see that Truffles and Jet were already heading in her direction. Holly did not want to share this smelly old ball with anyone.

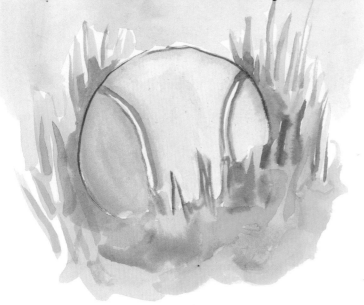

Discovering this old ball was like finding a treasure! She had to think of something quickly.

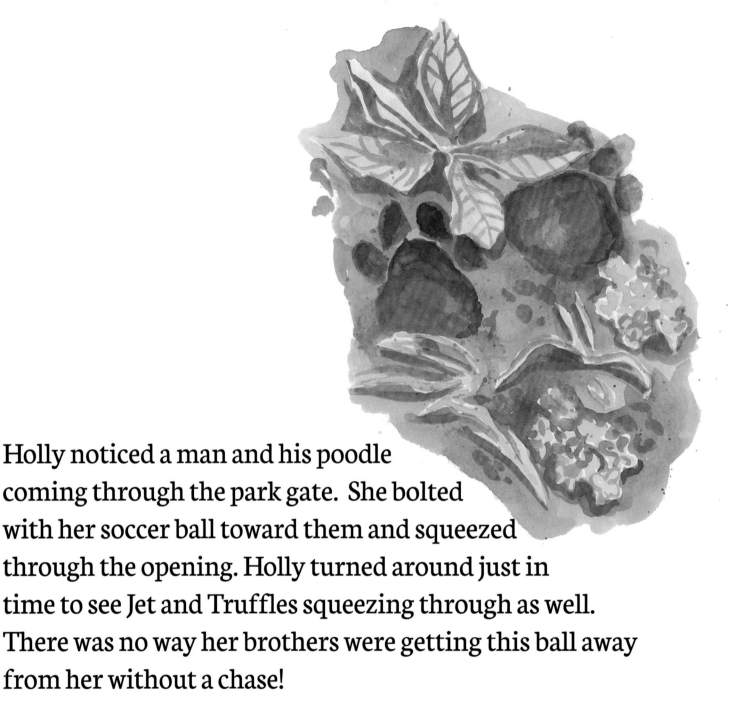

Holly noticed a man and his poodle
coming through the park gate. She bolted
with her soccer ball toward them and squeezed
through the opening. Holly turned around just in
time to see Jet and Truffles squeezing through as well.
There was no way her brothers were getting this ball away
from her without a chase!

Holly bounded down the path, crossed a field, splashed through a small creek and raced through a forest of trees. The ball was getting heavy and she could feel her legs getting tired.

A few seconds later, Truffles and Jet tackled Holly to the ground. They played tug-of-war with the ball until they were all too tired to move.

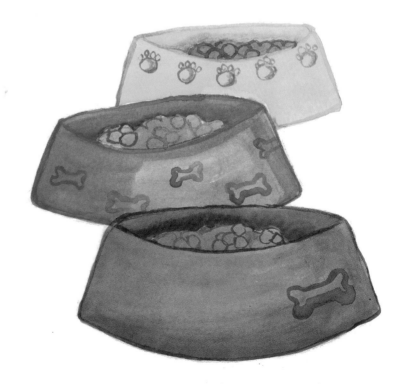

The three labs lay in a heap panting. Before long, they realized they were lost. They were lying in the backyard of a house they had never seen before.

They could not see Linda. They could not see the dog park. They could not see their dog van.

Holly quickly buried the ball and followed Jet toward the house. As they came closer, the dogs realized the back door had been left open. They noticed a delicious smell coming from inside the house.

Truffles pushed the door open wider and the dogs walked inside.

"Sniff, sniff!" To their surprise, sitting on the kitchen counter, were fresh baked muffins!

Truffles, Jet and Holly were just tall enough to reach the muffins and just hungry enough to gobble them all up. Soon the tray was empty and the labs were full!

The dogs were thirsty but they couldn't find a water bowl in the kitchen. Jet climbed the stairs to the bathroom where he found a large bathtub. Using a trick he had learned as a puppy, Jet pushed his paw against the faucet. The water turned on and the dogs had a nice long drink.

After their exercise, food and water there was only one thing left to do... the dogs would have a nice nap before finding their way back to the park. Upstairs the dogs found beautiful beds to race around and jump on. There were even lots of stuffed toys to play with.

After trying out all of the beds, the three labs settled down for a peaceful nap on the largest bed.

A short while later, the people who lived in the house came home.

"Mommy, where did you put all the muffins you made? The tray is empty!" asked a little girl's voice.

The voice continued, "Mommy... someone chewed my teddy bear and left pieces of it all over the stairs!"

The little girl climbed the stairs.

"Someone has messed up my bed, mom!" The girl's voice was shrill now.

The little girl heard the sound of running water. She peeked inside the washroom door.

"Eek!!! MOMMY! Someone has turned on the bathtub but there's nobody here!"

The little girl was now screaming, "THERE MUST BE A BURGLAR IN THE HOUSE!"

The little girl screamed so loud that she startled the three sleeping labs. They huddled together on the bed and tried not to make noise with their wagging tails.

The little girl ran toward her mother's bedroom. She entered the room and screamed the loudest scream she had ever screamed. "AAHHHHHHHH!!!!!"

There, in front of her, were three giant dogs curled up together on her mother's bed.

Now I ask you: "What would you do if you found three strange dogs on your mother's bed?"

In this story, the little girl looked from one dog to the next and the next, took one step backward, closed her eyes, and counted to ten.

When she opened her eyes, there were still three dogs sitting on her mother's bed. Her mother was standing at the bedroom door, her mouth wide open.

The little girl blinked and asked, "Are those dogs real?"

"I believe those three dogs are our burglars!" replied her mother.

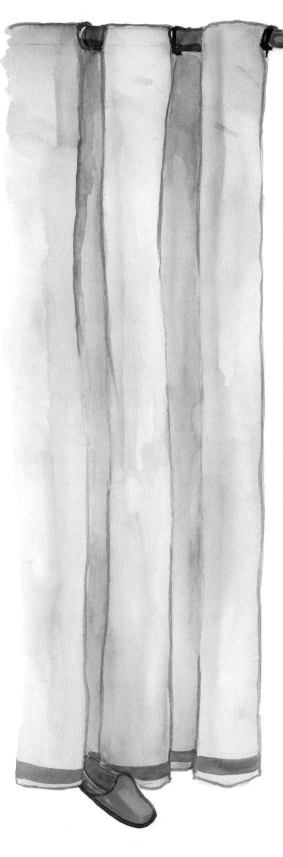

Holly, Jet and Truffles sat on the bed. They did their best cute dog look.

The little girl sat down on the floor in shock.

Her mother stood still, looking in dismay at the three dogs.

Just then the dogs heard a familiar sound.

They jumped off the bed, ran past the little girl and her mother, ran down the stairs to the front door of the house and began to whimper.

The mother and her daughter ran to the bedroom window. They spotted a van driving slowly by their house. On the side of the van were the words "HOME ALONE PET SERVICES".

The mother ran downstairs and opened the front door. She could hear the sound of barking coming from the van and she could hear a voice calling frantically out the window, "Truffles, Jet, Holly!"

In the next instant, the three burglars raced past the mother, out the door and straight toward the van.

Linda jumped out of the van and the three labs jumped in.

Linda looked at the dogs in disbelief, "What have you labs been up to?"

Truffles, Jet and Holly lay down on the floor of the van with their tails between their legs.

As the van drove off with the dogs safely inside, the loudest sound that could be heard was the sound of laughter coming from the home of the young girl and her mother. This was one crazy break-in they would never forget!